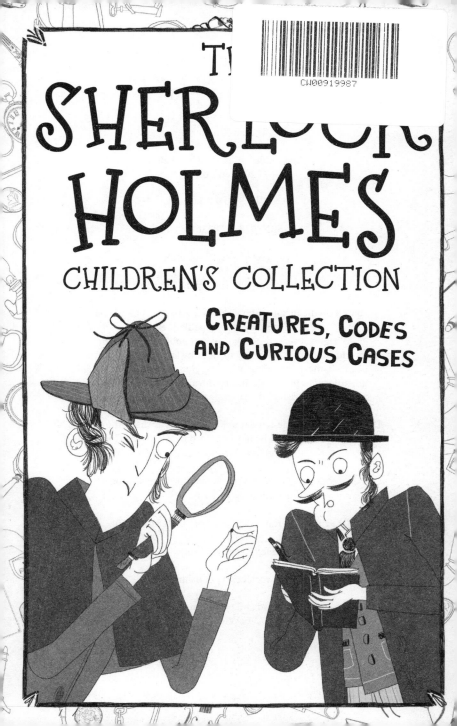

Published by Sweet Cherry Publishing Limited
Unit 36, Vulcan House,
Vulcan Road,
Leicester, LE5 3EF
United Kingdom

First published in the UK in 2021
2021 edition

2 4 6 8 10 9 7 5 3 1

ISBN: 978-1-78226-434-7

Sherlock Holmes: The Dying Detective

Based on the original story from Sir Arthur Conan Doyle,
adapted by Stephanie Baudet.

Cover design by Arianna Bellucci and Amy Booth
Illustrations by Arianna Bellucci

Lexile® code numerical measure L = Lexile® 650L

Guided Reading Level = W

www.sweetcherrypublishing.com

Printed and bound in China
C.WM004

SHERLOCK HOLMES

THE DYING DETECTIVE

SIR ARTHUR CONAN DOYLE

Chapter One

'Mr Sherlock Holmes is dying!'

I looked with horror at Mrs Hudson, the landlady of 221B Baker Street. She stood on the doorstep of my home in Latimer Square, where I now lived with my wife.

Mrs Hudson was agitated. She was wringing her hands and

pulling at her sleeves as tears poured down her face. Behind her was the hansom cab she had arrived in, waiting to take me back to Baker Street with her.

Hansom cab

A quick and relatively cheap mode of public transport, just right for two people. It can take corners fast without tipping over, despite having only two wheels. The driver sits outside at the back of the carriage, so that passengers are able to have a private conversation. Another choice is the Clarence cab. These have four wheels and are called 'growlers' because of the noise they make over cobbles. They are useful for groups of more than two, or if taking luggage.

'He's dying, Doctor Watson. For three days he has been getting worse. I don't think he will live through the night. He wouldn't let me get a doctor before today, but this morning when I saw how thin and weak he was, I insisted. He said it must be you.'

'I'll get my things,' I said, turning back inside. I grabbed my bag and pulled my coat

off its hook with such force that
I nearly tore a hole in its collar.
Then I said goodbye to my wife
and dashed out of the door.

Sitting in the cab, my mind
whirled with horrible thoughts.
Whatever was wrong? What had
happened? Holmes, my dear
friend, *dying?* I felt sick at the
thought.

The ride seemed endless despite
it being only a short distance. I
urged the driver to hurry.

Poor Mrs Hudson was in a state. Though he caused her endless trouble, Holmes was one of her dearest friends. She had put up with all his mess and chemical experiments, and who knows how many times she had to apologise to the neighbours for the funny smells, small explosions and sounds of gunfire coming from 221B Baker Street.

Not to mention the stream of people who came to see him. Some were respectable, but some were very suspicious-looking.

I turned to her and forced myself to smile. 'It's going to be all right, Mrs Hudson. Just tell me the details,' I said.

'There is not much I can tell you, sir,' she said, dabbing her eyes. 'He's been working in some alleyways down by the docks in South London and has caught an illness.

That's what he says. He went to bed

on Wednesday and hasn't moved

since. He hasn't had any food or

drink for nearly three days.'

Docks

An area of water, usually at the edge
of a river or sea, used for loading and
unloading boats, and repairing large
ships. The docks of Victorian London are
always busy. They are full of people, dirt,
disease and crime! Ships that have come
from across the globe, carrying goods
to England, can accidentally bring new
illnesses back too. Docks are also a good
place to look for criminals on the run –
many guilty people have fled to the docks
to board a ship to a distant land and
escape punishment.

I was horrified. 'You should have called a doctor earlier.'

'You know what a strong personality he has, Doctor Watson! I didn't dare disobey him until today.'

When we arrived at Baker Street, I soon saw for myself the horrid state Holmes was in.

In the dim light of the foggy November day, his bedroom was gloomy. Every corner looked grey and miserable, as if all its usual colour and life had been sucked from it. Holmes lay very still in his bed. The sight of his gaunt, thin face staring at me sent a chill to my heart.

His eyes were bright with fever and his cheeks were red. His skin looked dry and flaky, like ageing wallpaper, and dark crusts clung around his mouth. His thin hands twitched on the sheet. As I entered the room, there was a gleam of recognition in his eyes.

His croaky voice welcomed me. 'Well, Watson, something bad has happened to me,' he said. 'It seems I'm not indestructible after all.'

'My dear fellow,' I said as I went closer to the bed.

'Stand back! Stand right back!' His voice still had some of its sharpness. 'If you come near me, Watson, I shall order you out of the house.'

'Why?' I asked.

15

'Because I said so. Isn't that enough?'

Mrs Hudson was right. His strength of character was still there, even though his body was weak.

'I only wanted to help,' I said. 'I am a doctor. You should let me examine you.'

'No,' he said, and coughed loudly. 'You will help best by doing what you are told.'

'Certainly, Holmes.' I stepped back.

He relaxed.

'It's for your own sake, Watson,' he croaked.

'I've stood near many ill people, Holmes, as you know. I am only upset that you won't let me help you,' I said.

'I already know what is the matter with me. It is a disease from Indonesia. No one in England knows very much about it. But this is for certain: it is usually fatal and horribly contagious.'

Holmes
Mrs Hudson
Watson
Holmes is sick
Watson goes to
see him

Chapter Two

Holmes spoke with a feverish energy, his long hands jerking as he waved me away.

'It is contagious by touch, Watson. Keep your distance and all will be well.'

'Good heavens, Holmes! Do you think I'm worried about catching your sickness? Even if you were a stranger, I would want to help. Absolutely nothing would prevent me from helping my best friend.'

Again I stepped forwards, but he gave me a look as furious as thunder. 'If you stand back, I will talk to you. If you come any nearer, I shall order you from the room.'

Usually, I would do whatever Holmes asked, even if I didn't understand his reasoning. But not now. I could not ignore what my doctorly instincts were telling me.

'Holmes, you are not yourself,' I said. 'A sick person is like a baby – they do not understand what is best for them. Whether you like it or not, I am going to examine your symptoms and treat you for them.'

He looked at me with venomous eyes. His face contorted like a snake about to bite.

'If I have to have a doctor, whether I like it or not, let me at least have someone I trust.'

His words were like a knife in my heart. 'You don't trust me?'

'In your friendship, certainly. But facts are facts, Watson. You are only a family doctor, with very limited experience and average qualifications. It is painful to have to say these things, but I have no choice.'

I stood silently, stunned and terribly hurt by his words.

'I never thought you would say such things, Holmes. It shows very clearly how ill you are. But if you don't trust me, then let me fetch Sir Jasper Meek or Penrose Fisher. They are the best doctors in London and experts in contagious diseases. You *must* have someone treat you, and that's final. If you think I'm going to stand here and see you die without either helping you myself or finding someone else to help you, then you don't know me at all.'

I stood squeezing my hands

into fists to calm myself down after my strong speech.

'You mean well, Watson,' said Holmes with a groan. 'But my illness cannot be treated by any London doctor, I am sure of it. You can do nothing.'

'Perhaps I can't, but I know that Doctor Aintree, the world's greatest expert on tropical

diseases, is in London at the moment. No matter what you say, I am going to fetch him.' I stepped out of Holmes' bedroom, picked up my bag and turned to the door to the stairs, only to see – 'Holmes!'

In an instant, the dying man had sprung in front of me like a tiger. I heard the click of a key turning in the lock. Then he staggered back into his bedroom and onto his bed, exhausted and panting after the spurt of energy.

'I've got you, my friend. You won't take the key from me by force. You will stay in these rooms until I let you go,' he said between shaky breaths. 'I know you are thinking of me. Of course I do. You shall have your way, but not now, Watson. It's four o'clock. At six o'clock, you can go.'

'This is madness, Holmes!' I shouted.

'Only two hours, Watson. I promise you can go at six o'clock.

Are you willing to wait?'

'I seem to have no choice.' I
sat down in a chair at the end of
Holmes' bed, but could not relax.
How could we waste what little
time he had left? I felt so helpless.

'No, you're right, Watson. You have no choice at all,' he whispered, with a hint of the old twinkle in his eye. 'Now, when you do go for help, I insist that you do not go to the doctors you have mentioned. I must choose.'

'Of course,' I agreed.

'Those are the first two sensible words you have said since you came into the room,' Holmes said, smirking.

I sighed and rolled my eyes.

'Now,' he continued, before pausing to yawn. 'You will find some books in the sitting room if you need something to read. I feel like a drained battery so I'll take a nap. Then, at six o'clock, we will resume our conversation.'

watson wants to help or get a docter
Sherlock locks watson in room until 6

Chapter Three

I felt too restless to sit still or read. I got up from my chair and stood for a few moments looking at the silent figure in the bed. Holmes appeared to be asleep, his face almost covered by the sheet.

I wandered slowly into the sitting room, looking at the pictures of famous criminals that were stuck all over the walls. They brought back memories of some of the cases we had worked on together. There was Doctor Roylett, who killed his step-daughter with a deadly snake in order to have her money, and then there was the man who tried to smuggle a precious stone in the neck of a turkey. I sighed as I remembered our adventures.

Finally, I returned to Holmes' room. I was about to stoke the fire

when something on the shelf above
it caught my eye. The wooden
surface was completely covered
with pipes, notes, old newspapers,
gun cartridges and other debris.

But in the middle was a small
black-and-white box with a sliding
lid. It was oddly intriguing. I
stretched out my hand to pick it up.

'Arrrgghh!'

The dreadful cry cut through
the silence of the gloomy room
and woke up a neighbour's dog,

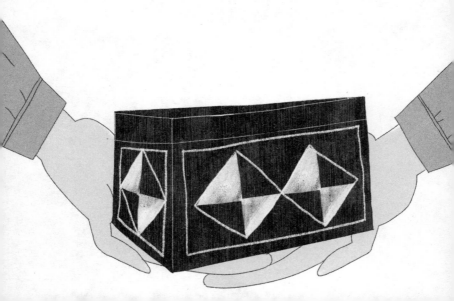

which barked loudly. I turned and caught sight of Holmes' frantic eyes and contorted face. One thin finger was pointing at the box in my hand.

'Put it down! This instant, Watson!'

Then, as suddenly as he had awoken, Holmes sank back down onto the pillow as if he were a deflated balloon. He gave a deep sigh of relief as I replaced the box on the mantelpiece.

'I hate people touching my things, Watson. You would drive anyone mad with your fidgeting. Sit down, man, and let me have my rest.'

This was so unlike Holmes. He would often snap at me if he was irritated, but his words were never this cutting.

I sat in silence, repeatedly looking at the clock and waiting for the hands to reach six o'clock.

Holmes must have been waiting, too, because the first

chime had barely rung when he began to talk. His voice was croaky and his hands darted about quicker than a hummingbird's heart beats.

'Now, Watson,' he said. 'Do you have any change in your pockets?'

'Yes,' I said. 'Quite a lot.'

'How many half-crowns?'

I delved into my pocket and brought out a handful of coins.

'I have five.'

'Ah, not enough, not enough! How very unfortunate,' said Holmes. 'But please put them into your pocket-watch pouch. Then put the rest of your change into your left trouser pocket.'

I did as he asked.

'Thank you. It will balance you better like that.'

I stared at Holmes, bewildered. This was madness!

'It's never a good thing to be unbalanced, Watson. Too many

coins in one pocket and you could topple right over.'

Holmes suddenly shuddered, as if a cold draft had stroked his spine. He made a small sound between a cough and a sob.

'Now light the gaslights, please, Watson. But be very careful only to have them half on. That is really important.'

I stood up and went to the two gaslights on the walls, striking matches and lighting the mantles

through the holes in
the glass globes. Then I
carefully pulled the little
chains to turn on the gas
supply, being sure to have
them no more than half on.

'Thank you, Watson,'
Holmes said when they
both glowed.

I went over to the
window to draw the blinds.

'No, please don't do
that. I want the blinds

left open. Now, please put some papers and letters on my table where I can reach them. Excellent! Oh, and that little box from the mantelpiece.'

When I had done all that, Holmes nodded.

'Now, please remove the lid of the box using the sugar tongs from our tea tray. Do not touch the lid with your fingers. Put it here amongst the papers. Good! You can now go and fetch Mr

Culverton Smith, at Number 13, Lower Burke Street.'

I had almost changed my mind about fetching a doctor by now. Holmes seemed so weak and confused that I thought it might be dangerous to leave him. I would have asked Mrs Hudson to watch him, but she was so upset already. I could still hear her sobbing down in the kitchen. But Holmes was insistent.

'I've never heard of Mr Culverton Smith,' I said. 'Are you sure he's the best doctor for the job?'

'He's not a doctor at all, my good Watson. You may be surprised to know that the most expert person in this disease is, in fact, a coffee grower.' He stopped to take a strained breath. 'Mr Smith is well known in Indonesia and is now visiting London. There was an outbreak of this disease on his plantation, but there were no doctors or hospitals anywhere nearby to treat it. So he studied the illness himself."

Holmes suddenly squeezed his eyes shut and gritted his teeth together as a spasm of pain took hold. When it passed, his face relaxed and he continued in a croaky whisper.

'I didn't want you to go for him until six o'clock because I knew he wouldn't be in his office. Mr Smith is a man of strict habits. But I'm sure he could help me. Please beg him to come and to use his unique experience of this disease to cure me.'

During the few hours I had been with Holmes, his face had changed for the worse. The red spots on his cheeks were darker and there was a blanket of sweat covering his forehead.

'Tell him exactly how ill I am, Watson' he said. 'Be honest. Tell him what you are thinking now – that I am a dying man. Dying and talking nonsense. See here – is the whole bed of the ocean covered with oysters? There are so many

of them that it must be true. Ah! My mind is wandering. Isn't it strange how the brain controls the brain? And every other body part, for that matter. Busy old brain … What was I saying, Watson?'

'My instructions for Mr Culverton Smith,' I said, looking at Holmes with utter confusion.

'Ah, yes. I remember. My life depends upon it. Plead with him, Watson. There is bad feeling between us. We are no longer friends. It was about his nephew, Watson. I suspected foul play and I let him know it. The boy died horribly. So beg him. Get him here by any means. Only he can save me!'

'I will bring him in a cab even if I have to carry him out to it,' I said.

'You will do nothing of the sort!' snapped Holmes. 'You will persuade him. And then you will come back here *before* him. Make any excuse not to come *with* him.

Don't forget that, Watson. Don't fail me. You have never failed me … Do oysters have any natural predators? If they do not, then will the world be overrun with oysters? Will they learn to live on land? No, no! How horrible that would be … Promise you will tell him how ill I am, Watson?'

'Yes,' I said, trying my best not to show my fear. 'Yes, I promise.'

Chapter Four

Reluctantly, I left Holmes. Every step across the carpet and out of the apartment felt heavy, as if my mind were telling me to stay.

As I walked down the stairs, I still had his silly words about oysters ringing in my ears. How tragic that such an intelligent man should be babbling nonsense.

Mrs Hudson stood at the
bottom of the stairs, dabbing
at her tears with a
handkerchief. She
muttered, 'Oh
it is so horrible,
Doctor Watson,
so horrible.
What shall we do if
we lose him?'

I simply patted her shoulder,
handed her a clean handkerchief
and walked out of the door.

As I stepped out into the foggy street, I looked up at the dimly lit window. I could faintly hear Holmes' high, thin voice chanting madly.

He had given me the key to his bedroom door and I brought it with me in case he decided to lock himself in. I slipped it into my waistcoat pocket and stepped to the kerb to whistle for a cab.

Suddenly a man appeared out of the fog. 'How is Mr Holmes, sir?' he asked.

It was an old friend of ours: Inspector Morton of Scotland Yard.

'He is very ill,' I answered.

The inspector looked at me in the strangest way. I thought I saw a gleam of delight in his eyes. But perhaps it was just a trick of the light from the street lamp above us.

'I had heard a rumour about him being sick,' he said. 'I thought I should check for myself. Such a shame.' Again, it looked as if he were hiding a smile.

I frowned and puzzled over
this for a moment, but just then
a hansom cab drove up. When it
stopped, I jumped in.

I gave the inspector a wave. 'I'll
give him your best wishes,' I said,
pulling the little doors closed
in front of me to keep out the
November chill.

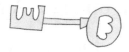

Lower Burke Street was lined
on both sides with rows of fine

houses. Number 13 was a large building with old-fashioned railings bordering the front garden. It had a huge double front door made of black wood, with a shining brass knocker and letterbox.

The moment my cab stopped and I got out, the door of Number 13 opened. A butler stood in the doorway with the pink glow of electric light behind him.

'I would like to see Mr Culverton Smith,' I said, mounting the steps. 'It's extremely urgent.'

'And who may I say is calling?' asked the butler.

'Doctor John Watson.'

My humble name did not impress the butler nor his master. Through the open door I heard a high, complaining voice. 'Who is this person? What does he want? Dear me, Staples, how often have I said that I do not want to be disturbed in my hours of study?'

'I am terribly sorry, sir. The man's name is Doctor John Watson. He would very much like to see you.' The butler's voice was gentle and soothing.

'Well, I won't see him,' said Mr Smith. 'I can't have my work interrupted like this. Say I am not at home. Tell him to come in the morning if he really must see me.'

Again, the butler gently murmured a reply. 'He looks rather upset, sir. It would be rude to turn him away.'

'I don't care how he looks, Staples. Just give him that message. He can come in the morning or he can stay away. My work must not be hindered.'

I thought of Holmes tossing in his bed, wracked with pain and fever, counting the minutes until I would arrive with help. It was not a time to be polite. His life depended on my quickness.

Before the apologetic butler could give me his master's message, I pushed past him into the hall, looking around for the room where Mr Smith's voice had come from.

Chapter Five

I found the room and threw the door open. With a shrill cry of anger, a man leapt to his feet from a chair in front of the fire.

He had a yellow face with course, greasy skin. His double chin shook and his angry grey eyes glared at me menacingly from under thick eyebrows.

He wore a blue velvet cap on his large head.

As I looked down at him, I saw that despite his large head, he was a very small, frail man with a curved spine.

'What's this?' he cried. 'How rude of you to burst in here! Didn't I say that I would see you tomorrow morning?'

'I am sorry,' I said, 'but the matter cannot be delayed. Mr Sherlock Holmes ...'

The mention of my friend's name had an extraordinary effect on the man. The angry look disappeared from his face in an instant.

'Have you come from Mr Holmes?' he asked.

'I have just left him.'

'How is he?'

I could not quite read the expression on his face. Was it one of excitement or worry?

'Not well,' I said.

'Please sit down.' Mr Smith pointed to a chair and then returned to his own.

As he did so, I caught a glimpse of his face in the mirror on the wall. I could have sworn that there was an evil smile lurking there, yet when he turned back

to me, his face was kind and caring. Was I imagining things? *Again?*

'I'm sorry to hear that Mr Holmes is not well,' he said. 'I only know him through some business dealings we had, but I know he is a good man, and a very talented one, too. He is an expert in crime as I am in disease. For him the villain, for me the virus.'

I nodded, wondering what business Holmes could have had with this man.

'There are my prisons,' Mr Smith continued, pointing to

a row of bottles and jars on a side table. 'In there, some of the world's deadliest bacteria and viruses are doing their prison sentences.'

I shuddered with horror at the thought. 'It is because of your special knowledge of illnesses that Mr Holmes wants to see you,' I said. 'He has a high opinion of you. He thinks you are the only man in London who could help him.'

Mr Smith jumped in shock. His hat fell off his head and onto the floor.

'Why?' he asked. 'Why would Mr Holmes think that I could help him?'

'Because of your knowledge of Eastern diseases,' I said.

'But how does he know that the disease he has caught came from the East?'

'Because he was working on a case down in the docks, where

there are a lot of ships and sailors from East Asia.'

Mr Smith nodded as he bent down to pick up his smoking cap.

'Oh, I see,' he said. 'How long has he been ill?'

'About three days.'

'Is he confused? Saying lots of odd things?'

'Yes. Now and again he lapses into babbling nonsense. His mind is definitely affected.'

He tutted. 'This does sound bad. It would be cruel not to go when he has asked for me. I do not like my work being interrupted, Doctor Watson, but this is an exceptional circumstance. I will come with you at once.'

I suddenly remembered that Holmes had insisted that I go back to Baker Street before Mr Smith.

I got up from my chair. 'I have another urgent appointment,' I said. 'But I shall get there as soon as I can.'

'Very good,' Mr Smith said. 'I will meet you there. Please write down his address for my coachman. My memory is bad. I shall be there within half an hour.'

He stood up and pushed a piece of paper and a pencil across the table towards me.

I wrote down the address and then said a speedy goodbye before rushing to the door.

It was with a sinking heart
that I hurriedly travelled back
to Baker Street. I knew that the
worst might have happened while
I was gone.

221B Baker Street

Chapter Six

Standing outside Holmes'
bedroom, I took a deep breath to
steady my nerves. Then I twisted
the handle and very slowly
pushed open the door.

'Hello, Watson,' came the voice
from the bed.

I let out the breath I had been
holding and immediately sank

into a chair. To my enormous relief, Holmes had improved while I had been out. He looked as ghastly as ever, but his mind was sharp. There was no trace of the confused, rambling man from before. His voice was still weak and croaky, but full of determination.

'Well, did you see him, Watson?' he asked.

'Yes. Mr Culverton Smith is coming.'

'Wonderful, Watson! Wonderful! You are the best messenger I could ask for.'

'He wanted to return with me,' I said, 'but I remembered your instruction.'

'That would never do, Watson. That would be impossible. It's good that you came back alone. Did he ask what was the matter with me?'

'Yes. I told him about your work in the docks, where all the ships from the East are moored. I said that's where you must have caught the disease.'

'Exactly! Well done, Watson. You have done all that a good friend could do. Now you must disappear.'

'Certainly not!' I said. 'I want to wait and hear his opinion, Holmes.'

'I know,' Holmes said, 'but I think his opinion would be much more honest if he thought we were alone. You do not have to leave, my friend. There is just enough room behind the head of my bed for you to hide.'

'Hide? My dear Holmes, that's utterly mad!'

'There is no other way, Watson. There's nowhere else to hide in this small room. Mr Smith won't suspect a thing.'

Suddenly Holmes sat up and craned his neck towards the

window. 'I can hear carriage wheels, Watson. Quick! If am truly your closest friend, then you will do as I say. Hide! And don't move, whatever happens – do you hear? Don't speak, don't move. Just listen.'

In an instant, Holmes' strength faded. Again, his voice transformed into the low murmurings of a confused man.

I quickly stepped behind the headboard of the bed and

crouched down. The gaslights
were only half on, so I hoped I
would not be seen.

I heard the front doorbell ring and then the hushed tones of Mrs Hudson welcoming someone in. Then there was a series of slow, careful footsteps coming up the stairs. The door creaked open. I could hear Mrs Hudson sniffling, before the door closed. The same slow footsteps approached the bed. I held my breath.

To my surprise, there was near-silence for a long while. I could imagine Mr Smith standing by the bedside, looking down at Holmes. What was the expression on his face now? I couldn't move to check.

At last the silence was broken.

'Holmes!' said Mr Smith. 'Mr Holmes!' His tone was insistent, as though he were trying to wake someone who was asleep. 'Can't you hear me, Holmes?'

There was a rustling of sheets, as if he had shaken my sick friend roughly by the shoulder.

'Is that you, Mr Smith?'
Holmes whispered. 'I didn't think
you would come.'

Mr Smith laughed.

'And yet, as you see, I am here,'
he said. 'I am not such a bad fellow
after all. You are my enemy and yet
I have come to help you.'

'It is very good of you,' said
Holmes. 'I appreciate your special
knowledge.'

Mr Smith sniggered. 'You are
the only man in London who

recognises that I have special knowledge. Do you know what is the matter with you?'

'It is the same illness that killed your nephew, Victor,' said Holmes.

'Ah, you recognise the symptoms?'

'Only too well.'

'Well, I wouldn't be surprised if it *were* the same. It's not good news if it is, though. Poor Victor was dead on the fourth day – and he was a strong and healthy young fellow. It was very strange that he caught a rare Asian disease in the heart of London. Even stranger that it was a disease that I had studied. Such a coincidence, Holmes.'

'I know what you did,' said Holmes.

'Oh, you do, do you?' said Mr Smith. 'Well, you

can't prove it. You have just spread nasty rumours about me instead and ruined my reputation. But now, when you are in trouble, you come crawling to me for help. What sort of a game is that, eh?'

I heard the rasping, laboured breathing of Holmes. 'Give me some water, please,' he gasped.

'You're very near your end, my friend. But I don't want you to die until I have had a word with you.

So, here, you can have some water.'

I heard the sound of Holmes struggling to sit up and sip from the glass. I desperately wanted to come out of my hiding place and comfort him during his last moments, but I had promised that I wouldn't.

'Don't spill it,' said Mr Smith, sharply. 'Can you understand what I'm saying?'

Holmes groaned. 'Yes, I understand. Please, do what

you can for me. Forget what has happened between us in the past. I'll forget everything I know – I swear. Please cure me and I'll forget it.'

'Forget what?'

'About Victor Savage's death. You almost admitted just now that you had caused it. I'll forget that I heard.'

'Yes, I killed him. But I do not care whether or not you forget that fact. You will not be testifying in the witness box in court. You will be in a different box soon, Holmes. I assure you.'

'Yes, I fear I will,' whispered Holmes, in a voice so weak I had to strain my ears to hear.

'The fellow who came to get me – I forget his name – said that you caught the disease down in the docks,' said Mr Smith.

'That's the only place I can think I would have caught it.'

'You are proud of your brains,

aren't you, Holmes? You think
you're smart. But you have met
someone who is smarter than
you. Think back, Holmes. Can
you think of another way you
could have got this disease?'

'I can't think. My mind has
gone. For heaven's sake, help me!'

I suddenly realised that I had
never seen Holmes so vulnerable
before. He was always so strong
and in control. My throat tightened
and I fought the urge to cry.

'Yes, I will help you. I will not cure you. But I will help you understand exactly how you got ill. I'd like you to know before you die.' Mr Smith's voice dripped with disdain.

'Give me something for the pain!' begged Holmes.

'Painful, is it? Yes, I remember people

screaming before they died. It causes terrible cramp, I believe?'

'Yes, yes, it is cramp. I feel like my bones are fusing together.'

'Well, as long as your ears work, that's all that matters. Listen now! Can you remember any unusual incident in your life around the time you became ill?'

'No, nothing,' said Holmes.

'Think again,' snapped Mr Smith.

'I'm too ill to think.'

'Well, then, I'll help you. Did anything come by post?'

'By post?' asked Holmes.

'A box, for example,' said Mr Smith.

'I'm fainting – I'm gone!'

'Listen, Holmes!' There was a guttural growl behind his high-pitched voice. Then I heard Mr Smith shaking poor Holmes. I was so angry. I could hardly stop myself from jumping out from my hiding place. I pressed my

fingernails into the palms of my
hands and felt a tear slide down
my cheek.

'You must hear me, Holmes!'
cried Mr Smith. 'You *shall* hear

me. Do you remember a small box? It came on Wednesday. You opened it – do you remember?'

'Yes, yes, I opened it,' said Holmes. 'There was a sharp spring inside it. Some joke ...'

'It was no joke, you fool!' Mr Smith spat. 'Who asked you to meddle in my affairs? If you had left me alone, I would not have hurt you.'

'I remember,' Holmes gasped. 'The spring made my finger bleed.

It was this box – this one here on the table.'

'That's the very one,' said Mr Smith. There was a quiet click as Mr Smith gently put the lid back onto the little box, and the sweeping sound of wood sliding down silk as he popped it into his coat pocket. 'There goes your

last shred of evidence, Holmes,'
he continued. 'But you have
the truth now. You can die with
the knowledge that I killed you.
You knew too much about what
happened to Victor Savage, so
I am sending you on the same
journey. You are very near your
end now, Holmes. I will sit here
and watch you die.'

Chapter Seven

Crouched behind the headboard of Holmes' bed, I could hear my sick friend murmuring.

'What's that?' asked Mr Smith. 'Turn up the gaslights? Ah, things are getting dark, are they? Yes, I'll turn them up so you can see better.'

I heard Mr Smith move quickly around the bedroom, turning

up the gaslights. The room soon became brighter.

'Is there any other little thing I can do for you before your death, my friend?' asked Mr Smith, spitting out the final word. 'Anything I can get for you?'

'A match and a cigarette.'

I nearly laughed out loud. Holmes was speaking in his normal voice! It was a little weak, but certainly the voice I knew.

There was a long pause and I imagined Mr Smith standing in silent amazement, looking down at Holmes.

'What's the meaning of this?' he said.

'The best way of successfully acting a part is to *be* the part,' said Holmes. 'For three days I have had almost nothing to eat or drink before that water you just gave me. Ah, here are some cigarettes.'

I heard the striking of a match. Then there were several footsteps coming up the stairs.

'Do I hear the footsteps of a friend?' said Holmes.

The door opened. 'Well, Holmes,' said the voice of Inspector Morton. 'Is it done?'

'All is in order and this is your man,' said Holmes.

'What is this all about?' came the panicked cry of Mr Smith.

An officer entered the room

and gave the usual cautions. 'I arrest you on the charge of the murder of Victor Savage,' he said. 'You have the right to remain silent, but anything you say may be taken down and used in evidence against you.'

'And you might like to add the attempted murder of Sherlock Holmes to the charges,' said my friend with a chuckle. 'Mr Smith was good enough to give our signal by turning up the gaslights for me, Inspector. And by the way, the prisoner has a small box in the right-hand pocket of his coat. I would advise you to remove it, but handle it very carefully. Do *not* open the lid.'

A moment later, Holmes said, 'That's it, thank you, Inspector. Put it down here. It may be evidence in the trial.'

There was a sudden rush and a scuffle, followed by a cry of pain.

'You'll only get yourself hurt if

you try to escape,' said Inspector Morton. 'Stand still, will you?' There was the click of the closing handcuffs.

'A nice trap!' snarled Mr Smith. 'But it proves nothing! Holmes asked me to come here to cure him, Inspector. I felt sorry for him and I came. Now he will probably pretend that I've admitted to his mad suspicions. You can lie as much as you like, Holmes. It's my word against yours.'

I stepped out from behind the bed.

'Good heavens!' cried Holmes. 'I had totally forgotten about you! My dear Watson, I owe you a thousand apologies. I don't need

to introduce you to Mr Culverton
Smith, do I? You met earlier this
evening.'

Mr Smith could now see that
the game was up. There had
been a witness to everything he
had said. His heavy

face was set in a scowl and his shoulders slumped as he was led out of the room by the officer.

I remembered then how I had seen Inspector Morton outside as I was going to fetch Mr Smith and had been surprised at the pleased look on his face. Now I knew why. He had been in on Holmes' plan from the start. At the agreed time, he had been waiting in the street for his signal to come up and arrest the man.

'Have you got a cab waiting, Inspector?' asked Holmes. 'I will follow you when I am dressed and give a statement at the police station.'

When Mr Smith and the police had left, Holmes finished his glass of water and ate a couple of stale biscuits that had been

sitting amongst the mess on the mantelpiece.

'Oh, I needed that,' he said as he washed and dressed. 'I had to look thin and ill so that Mrs Hudson would go and fetch you, and so that you would fetch Mr Smith. I hope you're not offended, Watson? You are not much good at pretending, and if you had known that I wasn't really ill you would not have been able to convince Mr Smith to come. It

was vital that he came. I'm sorry
for having worried you, though.'

'Your face looked so ghastly,
Holmes. I truly thought you were
dying.'

'Three days of fasting does not
improve one's beauty, Watson.
For the rest, a little oil on the
forehead to look sweaty, and
some special drops to make the
pupils of my eyes enlarge. Add
some blusher on the cheekbones
and crusts of beeswax around

the mouth, and you have the
appearance of a very sick man.
Then there was the occasional
talking nonsense about oysters
and half-crowns to complete

the picture of someone who was very sick and confused.'

'But why wouldn't you let me come near you, since there was no infection?' I asked.

'Is that not obvious, Watson? I knew that your sharp judgement as a doctor would soon see through my make-up. I may have looked weak, but my pulse and temperature were normal. At four metres away I could deceive you, but certainly no nearer.'

I sighed happily. Holmes did not think I was a terrible doctor after all. I should have suspected that this was all an act.

Idly, I reached out to examine the little box on the table.

'No, Watson! Don't touch that. If you look at it sideways, you can just see where a sharp spring, like a snake's tooth, shoots out as you open it. I expect it was a similar device that Mr Smith used to kill his nephew, poor Victor Savage.

He killed him so that he would inherit his property. It's a sad story.

'But I know that I have enemies, Watson, so I am always suspicious of any little packages that come in the post.

I had the idea of pretending that Mr Smith had succeeded in infecting me so I could get a confession out of him. I think my performance showed me to be a true artist. It may even be worthy of an award.'

I smiled at Holmes' lack of modesty.

Then there was a tap on the door. It opened to reveal Mrs Hudson looking utterly bewildered. When she saw

Holmes, she rushed forwards with a cry as if to fling her arms around him.

Holmes backed away and simply grasped her hands in his. 'I do apologise, Mrs Hudson,' he said. 'It was all an act in the name of justice.'

As she dabbed away tears of joy with an already soggy handkerchief, I realised that Holmes was completely unaware of the amount of pain and panic he had put us through.

'Please help me on with my coat, Watson. When we have

finished at the police station, I
think a meal at Simpson's would
be a good idea.'

I smiled and helped Holmes
with his coat.

THE EVENING STANDARD

8th November 1903

SHERLOCK HOLMES SAVES THE DAY ... AGAIN!

Mr Sherlock Holmes, the well-known consulting detective, has miraculously recovered from the tropical disease he was thought to have caught only days ago.

Despite his poor health, Mr Holmes succeeded in apprehending Mr Culverton Smith – a man accused of murdering his nephew, Victor Savage, in order to inherit his fortune.

Mr Holmes will stand as a key witness at Mr Smith's trial next month.

Sherlock Holmes

World-renowned private detective Sherlock Holmes has solved hundreds of mysteries, and is the author of such fascinating monographs as *Early English Charters* and *The Influence of a Trade Upon the Form of a Hand.* He keeps bees in his free time.

Dr John Watson

Wounded in action at Maiwand, Dr John Watson left the army and moved into 221B Baker Street. There he was surprised to learn that his new friend, Sherlock Holmes, faced daily peril solving crimes, and began documenting his investigations. Dr Watson also runs a doctor's practice.

To download Sherlock Holmes activities, please visit www.sweetcherrypublishing.com/resources